INSTANT AUDIO on your iPod, mobile device, or computer

This story can be best enjoyed when accompanied by the entertaining performance of Keith Torgan, the storyteller, and Barbara Siesel, the flutist (and voice of Green Golly).

To listen to the story on your iPhone, iPad, iPod, or on any Android device - and to enjoy the 10 beautiful classical works introduced in the story - you simply need to download the free **StorySticker** app.

DYBZKRBRRB

To use the **StorySticker** codes (on the left for the story and at the back of the book for the music), simply download the **StorySticker** app for your iOS or Android device. Following the prompts, scan the code (tap on the bear to initiate scanning) or enter the 10-letter **StorySticker** code. Once the code has been identified (it will beep), simply press the PLAY button. You can then either listen on the cloud (which requires Internet) or save it locallly on your device (which does not).

Alternatively, you can set up a free account at www.storysticker.com to listen on your computer by entering the letter codes below each image.

This wonderful introduction to classical music includes tidbits of renowned pieces throughout the story. Longer versions of these flute performances (accompanied by Jessica Krash on the piano) are encoded at the back of the book in separate tracks. S... **StorySticker** codes or enter the 10-letter code to ad... **StorySticker** library for repeated enjoyment.

to all the moms and dads
who read us to sleep
and free our minds
to dream great dreams

K.T., B.S., & S.L.L.

Special thanks to Randall Keith Horton and American Music Media
for supporting Green Golly from the very beginning – and to Evan Torgan,
whose strength, love, and compassion are an inspiration to all.

Green Golly
& her Golden
Flute

written and performed by
Keith Torgan & Barbara Siesel

illustrations by
Suzanne Langelier-Lebeda

Eifrig Publishing LLC
Berlin Lemont

Published by Eifrig Publishing,
PO Box 66, Lemont, PA 16851, USA
Knobelsdorffstr. 44, 14059 Berlin, Germany.

For information regarding permission, write to:
Rights and Permissions Department,
Eifrig Publishing,
PO Box 66, Lemont, PA 16851, USA.
permissions@eifrigpublishing.com, +1-888-340-6543

CD: All rights reserved © 2013 The Green Golly Project
212 East 13th street, New York, New York 10003
www.greengolly.com

Produced in cooperation with
The American Music Educational Television Project
142-14 Pershing Crescent, #3, Briarwood, New York 11435

Library of Congress Control Number: 2013937849

Torgan, Keith and Barbara Siesel
Green Golly & her Golden Flute /
by Keith Torgan and Barbara Siesel, illustrated by Suzanne Langelier-Lebeda

p. cm.

Paperback: ISBN 978-1-936172-61-0
Hard cover: ISBN 978-1-936172-62-7

[1. Juvenile Fiction - Fairy Tales - Adaptations 2. Music - Classical 3. Music - Children's]
I. Langelier-Lebeda, Suzanne, ill. II. Title: Green Golly & her Golden Flute

17 16 15 14 2013
5 4 3 2 1

Printed on FSC-certified recycled acid-free paper. ∞

Once upon a time there was a girl whose parents were *SO* hungry they gave her to a witch in exchange for

a plate of salad!

Can you believe that?
Salad!
A plate of salad!

Salad!
Greens!
Lettuce!

Clearly the better end of the bargain
went to the witch with the amazing
garden. Sounds dreadful, doesn't it?

Well, actually the witch loved the girl—
more evidently than the parents!!

She named the child **Green Golly** for the golly good greens that in her garden grew!

As the girl grew she became more and more beautiful, so beautiful that all the young gentlemen paid a little too much attention to her.

And this concerned the witch …

And so the old hag put the girl in a very
tall tower with no doors and no stairway
and only a small circle of windows
from which to see the world.

Green Golly had nothing
to do all day long but
look at the view
and grow hair.

RAPUNZEL

ORDER REJECTED

TOWER BUILDERS INC.

Now, most children would have been miserable in that predicament.

But not Green Golly.

I'm so happy! Happy! Happy! I'm so happy! Happy, hap, hap, hap, hap, happy, happy, happy!

She was delighted! You see, the mountains changed with the seasons—from white with snow, to popping with flowers, to the deep dark greens of summer, to the blazing reds, yellows and oranges of fall—and of course all sorts of wonderful creatures wandered, crawled, and flew by. Green Golly was so delighted by everything she saw, she couldn't help but sing!

Green Golly,

Green Golly,

let down
your
hair

to
me.

*I*t's a good thing the girl had so much time to grow hair, because frankly it was the only way up to the tower. The witch climbed Green Golly's amazingly strong braid of hair. When she got to the top of the tower she said,

I've got something special for ya—think you're gonna like it.

And she took out a
beautiful golden flute.

Here ...   play this.

... Now maybe
we'll get some
rest from that
wretched voice
of hers.

Day in and day out, Green Golly played upon her golden flute. And as you can hear, the more she played, the better she sounded.

14

*W*hen snowflakes flew, she played … when flowers popped, she played … in the deep dark greens of summer, she played … and with the falling leaves, she played.

One day the old witch called out,

Green Golly! Green Golly! Let down your hair to me!

Up that great rope of braid the old maid shimmied.

Well young lady . . . I think it's time to move on.

You mean I can leave the tower?

No, not that.

Move on to more interesting music.

The witch took out a huge
stack of sheet music.

Music?
Music?!
I need
friends,
not
music!

These,
my daughter,
are the works of
the world's great
composers. I think
they'll make you
very happy.

But that was not to be.

Moe's Art???

Mouse Art???

MOZART!!!

Of course, being the kind of girl who could always make a pocketbook from a pig's ear, lemonade from a lemon, or fertilizer from a small pile of doo-doo…

she took out the first piece of music…

…and played.

As she played, the first star of evening appeared.

*T*he sky filled with stars … beautiful
sparkling stars as far as the eye could see.

One day, a handsome prince came galloping through the woods, when he heard music.

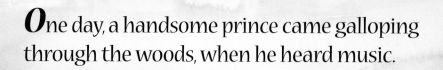

My, thought the prince. That sounds like "Spring Song" by Felix Mendelssohn!

Even though he was on an expedition for his father, the king, he just had to find out where that music was coming from.

I just have to find out where that music is coming from.

And who could be making such magical sounds.

Who could be making such magical sounds?

*H*e wandered over to the tower, but to his chagrin he discovered there was no door, no ladder, nothing. He called up ,

Yoohoo!

Yoohoo!

Yoohoo!

Green Golly was so busy practicing the flute, she didn't hear his sweet voice.

In frustration,

I'm so frustrated!

and because he was on an expedition for his father, the king, he mounted his steed and galloped away.

*H*ad Green Golly any
idea at all that such
a sweet prince had
stopped to listen and
wanted to meet her,
surely she would have
dropped her tresses!
Had she any idea at
all that such a man
had come and gone,
an arrow of gladness
would have pierced her
lonely heart. Because,
you see, even though
she loved her music and
she loved the view, she
was really quite lonely.

Lonely,

lonely,

lonely,

lonely

…lonely,

Lonely!

Lonely!

Lone–ly!

*I*n fact she was so lonely she didn't know what to do with these feelings—but then— it struck her! She would do what any great artist would do. She went over to her huge stack of sheet music, and she selected the piece of music that perfectly fit her feeling.

LONELY LONELY

SAD AND LONELY

WISTFULLY LONELY

And so she played the wistfully lonely *"Intermezzo Sinfonico"* from the opera *"Cavalleria Rusticana"* by Mascagni.

All of a sudden, a huge bumblebee flew into the tower. For some reason, the big fuzzball must really have liked the music, because he kept landing on the end of Green Golly's golden flute.

She wasn't frightened, she wasn't scared—
she was thrilled, she was inspired!

As the bee flew out the window, he turned to
Green Golly and said,

Wow! That was really good! Who wrote it?

Nicolai Rimsky Korsakov.

Of course-a-kov!

Bye!

Bye!

*W*ell, the next day … or it might have been the next year … nobody really knows … as Green Golly was busy tooting her flute by sunset, there appeared outside her window what may have been a band of gypsies.

Hello dere! You dere up in tower! Young lady! Dat is great tune you got dere. I tawt maybe you'd like to join my gypsy band and see da vorld. Va da you say?

Green Golly's heart leapt with delight. This could be her big chance. She ran to the window, she looked down, and what she saw was …

GREEN GOLLY AND HER GOLDEN FLUTE

26

… an ugly little man with a big guitar.

Where's the band, little man?

Band? Band. Oh, oh ho, ho, ho …
vell dere is not exactly band. It
is just me and Suzettska.

Suzettska? I don't see anyone.

Vell - Suzettska is vat I call
guitar. Anyvay, I tawt maybe
you'd like to play a tune or
two vit me. Vat is your name?

My name is Green Golly.

Ohhh, Green Golly, dat is very nice—I like dat.
Green Golly, Green Golly, is very . . .
Oh, ho, ho, ho, ho. Oh I am so sorry—
I am forget to introduce
myself for you.

I am

Vlotec,

the gypsy.

Happy to meet you,
Vlotec, the Gypsy.

No, happy to meet you,
Green Golly.

Well . . . what would you
like to play?

Do you know tune called "Habenera"?
It is from Carmen, by Bizet.

Well, umm . . . let me see if I have the
music.

*G*reen Golly was so excited . . .
she'd never played with anyone before.

Here it is. What do we do? How do we start?

Oh, ho, ho, ho. Dat vas so beautiful—ha, ha, ha.
You fill my heart—hee, hee, hee, hee, hee. Vould
you like to go out for date vit me?

Uh, well, um, Mister Vlotec, I'd really like to,
but, um, uh, I have to wash my hair tonight.

Now, to tell you the truth, Vlotec, the Gypsy,
was not really her type … he was very skinny
and very wrinkly and very old … he was
at least ninety-seven years old—maybe a
hundred and ninety-seven … nobody really
knows.

Um … if you're ever in this neck of the woods again
though … maybe we can play another tune.

Oh. Okay.
Dosvedanya!

Bye!

And so, Vlotec, the Gypsy, went his way.

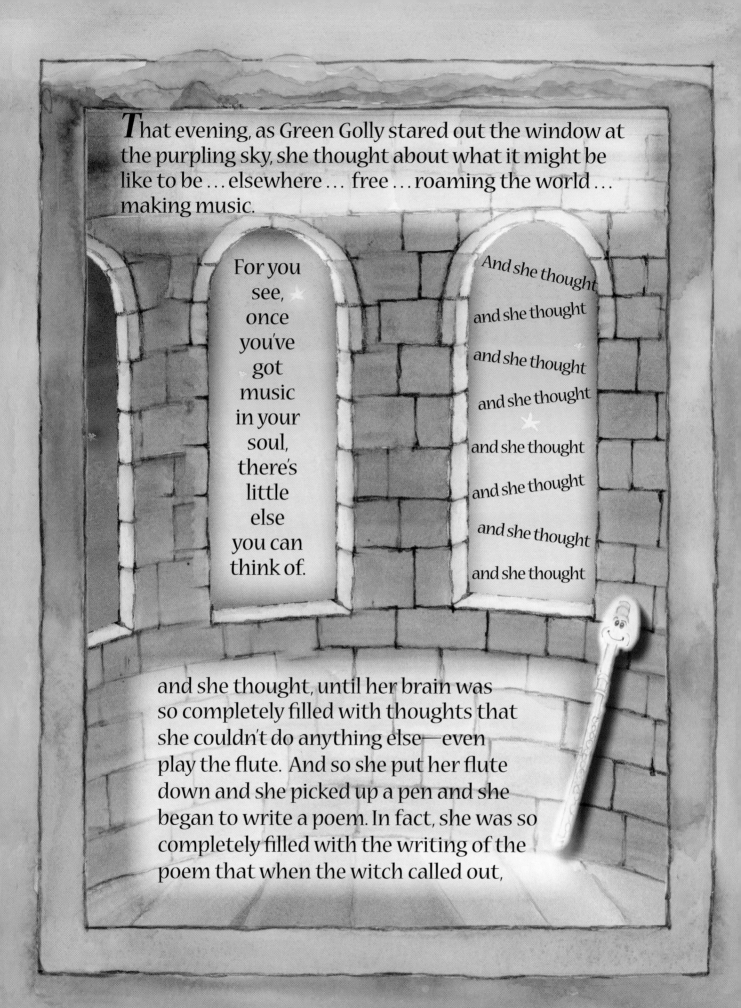

That evening, as Green Golly stared out the window at the purpling sky, she thought about what it might be like to be … elsewhere … free … roaming the world … making music.

For you see, once you've got music in your soul, there's little else you can think of.

And she thought and she thought and she thought and she thought and she thought and she thought and she thought and she thought

and she thought, until her brain was so completely filled with thoughts that she couldn't do anything else—even play the flute. And so she put her flute down and she picked up a pen and she began to write a poem. In fact, she was so completely filled with the writing of the poem that when the witch called out,

Green Golly, Green Golly, let down your hair to me!

she didn't hear a thing.

Green Golly, Green Golly, let down your hair to me!

Still there was no response.

Where is that girl?

The witch was worried.

Something must be wrong.

Green Golly never ignores me.

Once again, the witch called out ...

Green Golly!
Green Golly!
Let down your hair to me!!!!

All of a sudden a huge braid came flopping down over the side of the tower. It practically hit the hag in the head.

Ow! Uh, heh, heh, heh, heh, heh, heh, heh. There's ... heh, heh, heh. There's got to be a better way.

Once again, the old witch climbed Green Golly's amazingly strong braid of hair.

When she got to the top of the tower, she noticed that Green Golly didn't have her usual sparkle on. No music emanated from the soul of Green Golly.

What's the matter?

Nothing.

Nothing? That, that face does not look like nothing. What is it?

Nothing!

Nothing? What is you writing?!

Nothing!!

35

The witch grabbed the flute away from the girl, and she played it herself with such great passion that Green Golly could scarcely believe her ears!

Who's there?
What's that?

I am Mousey Tongue, famous talking mouse.

Never act out on raw emotion.

When one is angry one must step
back and consider all that is good
in life, and if that doesn't work,
sing a silly song!

Give me an "A" please!

Everyone repeat after me!
Me, me, me, me, me, me!

Never ever let yourself get in a hole
Look around and see if you can see the sun
Life is full of difficulties, but you know
You can have some fun

You are sure to have yourself the best of time
If you let yourself look at the happy things
Other people want you to be miserable
You mustn't let them win…

You take it, Miss Golly!

Isn't it delightful to be cuckoo mad
Better to be nutty than be miserable
Do a silly dilly. Brblbrblbrb!!!! Do a doofy dance
'Til you can't hide your smile.

*T*he little fellow bowed reverentially and said,

Remember . . . when you feel sad, sing a silly song.

And he disappeared through a crack in the wall.

Green Golly was so excited. That funny little Mousey Tongue fellow and his ridiculous little song kept her from smashing her golden flute and losing that which was most important to her.

I'm so happy I could dance!

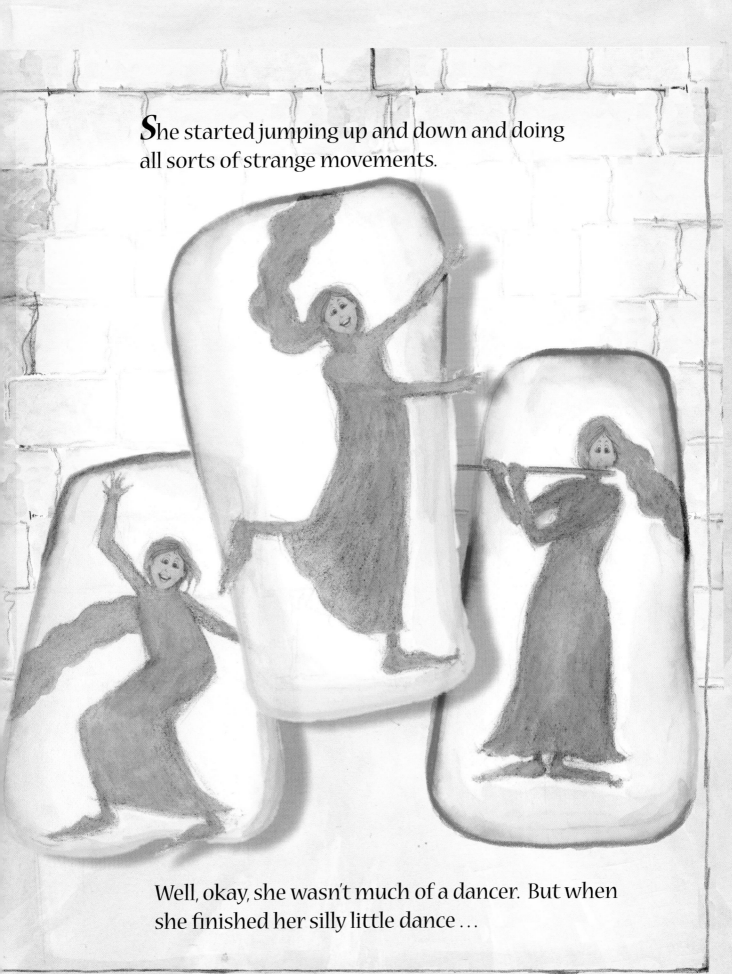

She started jumping up and down and doing
all sorts of strange movements.

Well, okay, she wasn't much of a dancer. But when
she finished her silly little dance …

...she picked up her flute again ...

... and she played the
fabulous
"Minute Waltz"
by Chopin.

There was just one problem. Green Golly had spent so many years in the tower studying music and practicing the flute, that when it came to certain things, she just didn't have a clue!

How does that witch get up here???

What is it the witch says when
she wants to get up to the tower?
Okay—I'll tell you. Everyone
repeat after me, but you have
to do it in a witch's voice!

Green Golly!

Green Golly!

Green Golly!

Green Golly!

Let down your hair to me!!

Let down your hair to me!!

Oohhh.
Hair!

And so Green Golly took her golden flute, her huge stack of sheet music—slipped it into a big black bag, slipped the bag over her shoulder, ran to the window, and threw out her long long hair . . .

This was a terrible idea—
and so she pulled her hair
back in the window. She
looked around the tower
until she discovered a pair of
scissors!

She cut off her braid of hair—
she tied it around a big old
nail in the tower—threw her
hair out of the window—
picked up her bag—

and slid down her own
hair to freedom!

Green Golly and her
Golden Flute went
off to see what they
could see.

THE END??

NOT EXACTLY!

*D*o you remember the prince? Well, one day, the prince was galloping through the woods once again when he came upon the tower. And he was hoping to hear music—but there was none. He got off his horse, and he walked over to the tower, and there was a note on the tower, and the note said …

Gone on tour. For more information, visit my website: www.greengolly.com andhergoldenflute

As the disappointed prince mounted his steed—the old witch came out—and she saw the prince and she saw the note and she thought to herself …

I deserve more …
I deserve love …
I deserve a second chance!

And so—being a witch—she turned herself into a beautiful young maiden.

When the prince saw her, he fell madly in love, and whisked her away to his kingdom, where they were wed and lived out their years!

I shoulda thought of this years ago!

POOF!!!

POOF!!!

POOF!!!

POOF!!!

POOF!!!

POOF!!!

POOF!!!

Of course, no wedding would be complete without music, and so they went to Green Golly's website, and they hired her to play for their wedding!

The old witch—now the beautiful young queen—listened on in delight…

… knowing that somehow, in spite of her past jealousy and over-protectiveness, she had somehow done a very good thing.